THE TROUBLEMAKER

Lauren Castillo

CLARION BOOKS
Houghton Mifflin Harcourt
Boston   New York

CLARION BOOKS
215 Park Avenue South, New York, New York 10003

Copyright © 2014 by Lauren Castillo

All rights reserved. For information about permission
to reproduce selections from this book, write to Permissions,
Houghton Mifflin Harcourt Publishing Company,
215 Park Avenue South, New York, New York 10003.

Clarion Books is an imprint of Houghton Mifflin Harcourt Publishing Company.
www.hmhbooks.com

The art was done in pen and ink with acetone transfer and compiled digitally.
The text was set in Fifteen 36.

LIBRARY OF CONGRESS CATALOGING-IN-PUBLICATION DATA

Castillo, Lauren, author, illustrator.
The troublemaker / by Lauren Castillo.
pages cm
Summary: After playing a trick on his sister by stealing her toy bunny,
a mischievous little boy wonders who the new troublemaker is when
his toy raccoon disappears.
ISBN 978-0-547-72991-6 (hardcover)
[1. Behavior—Fiction. 2. Lost and found possessions—Fiction. 3. Toys—Fiction.]
I. Title.   PZ7.C2687244Tr 2013
[E]—dc23
2012039686

Manufactured in China
SCP 10 9 8 7 6 5 4 3 2 1
4500459792

$16.99

JUN 2014

For Rachel, Megan, Becky, and Chad
(who are most certainly NOT troublemakers!)
—L.C.

I was bored.
Everyone else had something to do.

I know, Rascal. Let's play a game of pirates.

But we have to be *very* sneaky.

We'll need some rope,

a blindfold,

and a prisoner!

Now we send the prisoner out to sea.
Arrr! Off ye go, matey!

Mom found out
and she was NOT happy.

"No more taking your sister's things.
What do you say?"

I was playing nicely with my own toys

when I heard Mom calling.

But they didn't believe me.

"Stay here in the garden, where I can keep
an eye on you."

Rascal and I were collecting tomatoes for my boat.

But when I turned around, he was GONE!

And my boat and pirate hat disappeared too.

I wanted to look for Rascal, but Mom said
I had to wait until morning.

I bet Sister misses Bunny, too.

Hope they're okay.

When I woke up in the morning,
my blanket was missing!

I heard something, and when I looked outside, I saw the thief.

A sneaky raccoon!

What a troublemaker!